The Helpers in Your Neighborhood

By Alexandra Cassel Schwartz
Poses and layouts by Jason Fruchter

Simon Spotlight
New York   London   Toronto   Sydney   New Delhi

SIMON SPOTLIGHT
An imprint of Simon & Schuster Children's Publishing Division
1230 Avenue of the Americas, New York, New York 10020
This Simon Spotlight edition August 2019
Text and illustrated art © 2019 The Fred Rogers Company
Cover stock image: altrendo images/altrendo/Getty Images
Interior stock images: p. 10: Michael Warren/iStock/Getty Images; p. 11: Budimir Jevtic/Shutterstock;
p. 12: monkeybusinessimages/iStock; p. 13: ablokhin/iStock; p. 14: LightField Studios/Shutterstock;
p. 15: shironosov/iStock; p. 16, 24-25, 27: kali9/E+/Getty Images; p. 17: manonallard/E+/Getty Images;
p. 18: Weedezign/iStock; p. 19: FatCamera/E+/Getty Images; p. 20-21: hedgehog94/iStock;
p. 22: Blend Images - Don Mason/Getty Images; p. 23: dkapp12/iStock; p. 26: Marje/E+/Getty Images;
p. 28-29: Westend61/Gettyimages; p. 30-31: viavado/iStock
SIMON SPOTLIGHT and colophon are registered trademarks of Simon & Schuster, Inc.
For information about special discounts for bulk purchases, please contact Simon & Schuster
Special Sales at 1-866-506-1949 or business@simonandschuster.com.
Manufactured in China 0619 LEO
10 9 8 7 6 5 4 3 2 1
ISBN 978-1-5344-4322-8 (hc)
ISBN 978-1-5344-5208-4 (pbk)
ISBN 978-1-5344-4323-5 (eBook)

"*Wee-oo! Wee-oo!* Hi, neighbor! Have you ever seen anyone wearing a helmet like this?" Daniel asks. "I'm a firefighter." Daniel is pretending to be the different helpers in his neighborhood.

Now Daniel is pretending to be a crossing guard.
"Stop," Daniel tells Dad Tiger.
Dad waits for Daniel's signal.
"Now you may go," Daniel says.

"Grr-ific idea!" says Daniel. He and Dad hop on Trolley, buckle their seat belts, and head out of the Neighborhood of Make-Believe.

Daniel spots construction workers up ahead. "I wonder what they are building," he says.

They are working on a new apartment building! "Many people will live there when the building is done," Dad says.

The Tigers wave and continue walking.

Oh no! Daniel just took a tumble on the sidewalk. He feels okay, but Dad wants to be sure.

"What should we do?" Daniel asks.

Dad says, "In times like these, we look for the helpers."

Daniel sees a helper. "A police officer!" he says. The police officer patrols the neighborhood to make sure everyone is safe. He knows where Daniel and Dad can go for help.

The police officer gives Daniel and Dad directions to the next helper. Can you guess who the helper is?

Daniel meets a doctor!

"Hi, Daniel. It's nice to meet you," he says. "Doctors, nurses, and dentists help people who are hurt or sick feel better."

Daniel and Dad tell the doctor about Daniel's fall. The doctor gives Daniel a checkup. Daniel is healthy and strong.

Daniel knows that red means "stop" and green means "go." The crossing guard helps in the neighborhood by using a red stop sign to tell the drivers of the cars to stop. When the cars stop, people can safely cross the street.

The crossing guard is helping students cross the street to school. Daniel loves school. "I can't wait to see what school is like in this neighborhood," he tells Dad.

"Why, hello," says the teacher. "In this school we learn something new every day. I love being a teacher and helping students learn."

"Just like *my* teacher, Teacher Harriet!" Daniel exclaims.

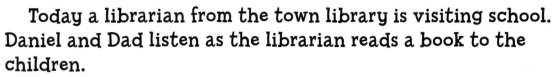

Today a librarian from the town library is visiting school. Daniel and Dad listen as the librarian reads a book to the children.

"This reminds me of when X reads to us in our neighborhood library," Daniel says to Dad after the story is finished.

Now it's time to play outside! But when the students get to the playground, they see a big mess. Last night there was a lot of wind, and it blew trash onto the playground.

"Let's help clean up," Dad suggests to Daniel.

An environmental services worker picks up the garbage bags and drives them away in a big truck!

Daniel loved seeing the school in this neighborhood, but he and Dad have other places to visit. As they walk down the street, Daniel spots a place where lots of helpers work. Do you know who they are?

They're firefighters! Firefighters wear heavy clothing to protect them when they put out a fire, just like these firefighters who show Daniel around the firehouse.
"I have a pretend firefighter helmet!" Daniel tells them.

One of the firefighters shows Daniel a fire truck up close!

"*Wee-oo! Wee-oo!*" Daniel says. He pretends he is driving the fire truck and sounding the siren.

Then Daniel notices a different kind of truck. "What kind of truck is that?" he asks.

"This is an ambulance," says Dad.

Paramedics help people when they are hurt or sick by taking care of them on the way to the hospital. The paramedics give Daniel and Dad a tour of the ambulance. They show them all the different equipment they use to help people.

Helpers come in all shapes and sizes. Dad and Daniel even visit a dog and her trainer! "That puppy is a helper?" Daniel asks.

"She sure is," says the trainer. "I am training her to be a guide dog. When she is ready, she'll know how to lead people who cannot see or have trouble seeing to where they are going."

Daniel and Dad join the trainer and the puppy for a walk.

As they walk, Daniel and Dad spot Trolley. It is starting to get late.

"Time to head home," says Dad.

"We met a lot of helpers today," says Daniel.